The Last Garden

Rachel Ip • Anneli Bray

Hodder
Children's
Books

In the middle of our country there was a city.

In the middle of the city there was a garden.

The city was grey and sad, but the garden was bright and beautiful.

Once, before the war came, there were trees on every corner.

Now, this was the last garden left.

The war went on, and still Zara looked after her garden. There were pear trees and nut trees and flowers and herbs.

Zara grew figs and apricots and all kinds of
vegetables for the people of our city.

She let us climb trees and build dens.

Sometimes we picked fruit and
helped her water the plants.

We took Zara's flowers home to our broken houses.

We brought her figs and pears
to our friends in hospital.

But the war was
on our doorstep.

Bombs

were

falling

and our

homes

shook.

There were cracks in our road and the wall around our playground crumbled.

We no longer played in our playground, but we still enjoyed Zara's garden. She showed us how to tie up her broken plants, and we picked the bruised and tender vegetables.

Together, we planted new seeds in old tin cans
and rusty paint pots. Greyness and sadness had spread
through our city, but our plants grew green and bright.

Then one day, we weren't allowed in Zara's
garden any more. It wasn't safe to play outside.

Bombs were falling every day and nowhere was safe in our city. Everyone was leaving. We packed up our things because we were leaving too.

Zara locked the gate to her garden
and we left our city together.

For months, Zara's garden
lay empty and alone.

But it was still growing . . .

At last, the day came when the war was over.

Slowly we returned to our broken city.

Zara still had the keys to
her garden. She unlocked the gate.

Zara smiled. All those months
her plants had still been growing!

They were tall and
strong and wild
and free.

Her garden was full
of life and colour.

Just as before, we went to play in Zara's garden.

We climbed trees and picked pears.

We helped Zara water the flowers.

And like the garden, our city blossomed
and came back to life.